For Dr. R. Maurice Boyd
(whose words taught us to fly)

Printed in Malaysia

First edition
1 3 5 7 9 10 8 6 4 2

H106-9333-5-14258

Library of Congress Cataloging-in-Publication Data

Kirsch, Vincent X., author, illustrator.
Freddie & Gingersnap find a cloud to keep / words & pictures by
Vincent X. Kirsch. —First edition.
pages cm
Summary: When Freddie the dinosaur and Gingersnap the dragon
climb up high hoping to meet a cloud, they find a very curious one, indeed,
and while they cannot keep it, it does leave them with something special.
ISBN 978-1-4231-5976-6 (alk. paper)
[1. Clouds—Fiction. 2. Dinosaurs—Fiction. 3. Dragons—Fiction.]
I. Title. II. Title: Freddie and Gingersnap find a cloud to keep.
PZ7.K6383Ft 2015
[E]—dc23   2013045911

Text is set in Farao
The artwork was created using watercolor, matte medium,
black gesso, cut paper, and lots of glue.

Reinforced binding

Visit www.DisneyBooks.com

FREDDIE & GINGERSNAP FIND A CLOUD TO KEEP

Vincent X. Kirsch

Disney • HYPERION

LOS ANGELES   NEW YORK

Gingersnap and Freddie were on their way to meet a cloud when Freddie asked, "If we meet a cloud, may I keep it?"

"Sorry to say," said Gingersnap, "no one can keep a cloud!"

At the top of the sky, there wasn't a cloud to be seen,
but Freddie heard a faraway song.

"What about a cloud like that?" he asked.

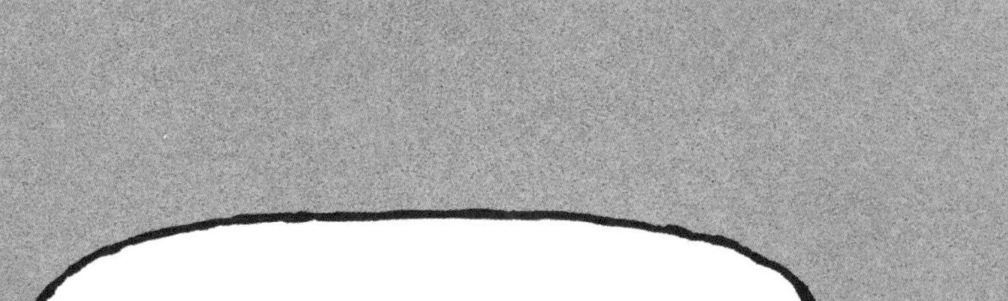
FARTHER AND FURTHER!
HIGHER AND HIGH!

"No matter what kind it is," said Gingersnap,
"no one can keep a cloud!"

"But *that* cloud is looking for a home!"
Freddie explained.
"I have a home. May I keep *that* cloud?"

"Clouds don't have homes,"
Gingersnap replied.
"And anyway, no one can keep a cloud!"

"But it seems like such a friendly cloud," said Freddie.
"Maybe I can keep it for a little while!"

"Not even for a little while.
You cannot keep a cloud,"
said Gingersnap. "But . . ."

"But this cloud does ask a lot of questions!
I have never met one like that before!"

"What did the cloud say?" Freddie asked.
"Are we dangerous? Do we like to eat children?"

"What does *dangerous* mean?" Gingersnap asked.
"What are *children*?"

"Magic?" said Gingersnap.

"What's that?" said Freddie.

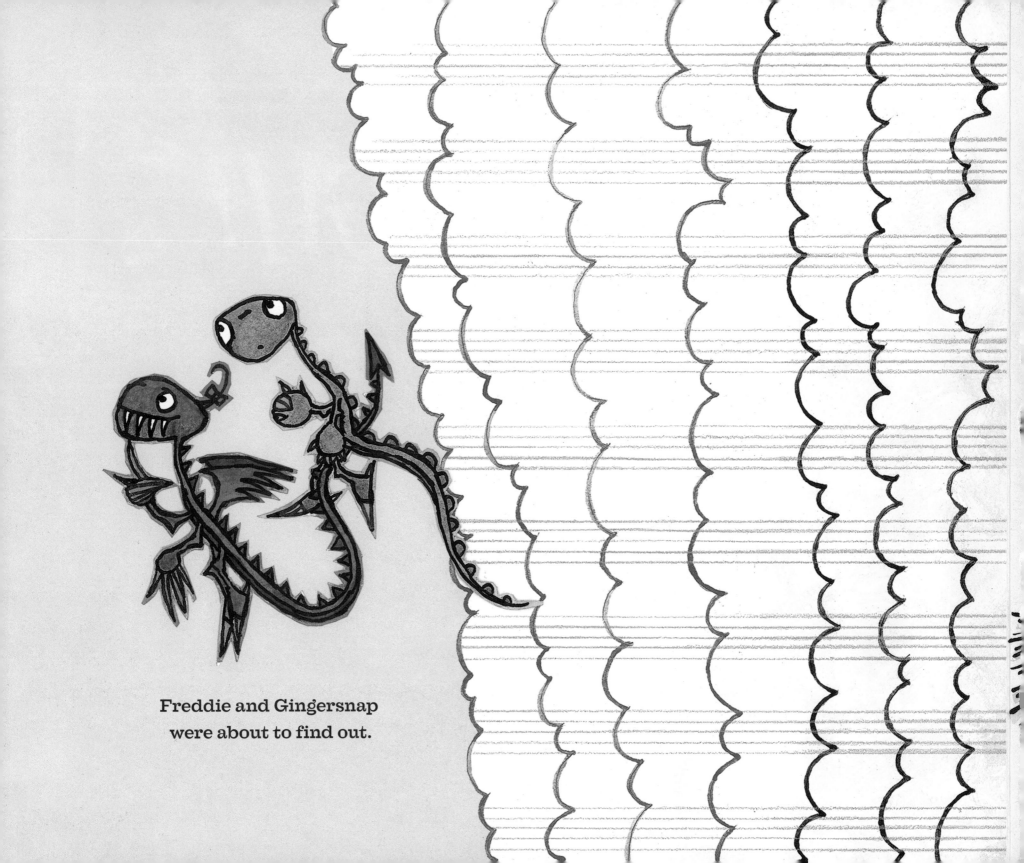

Freddie and Gingersnap
were about to find out.

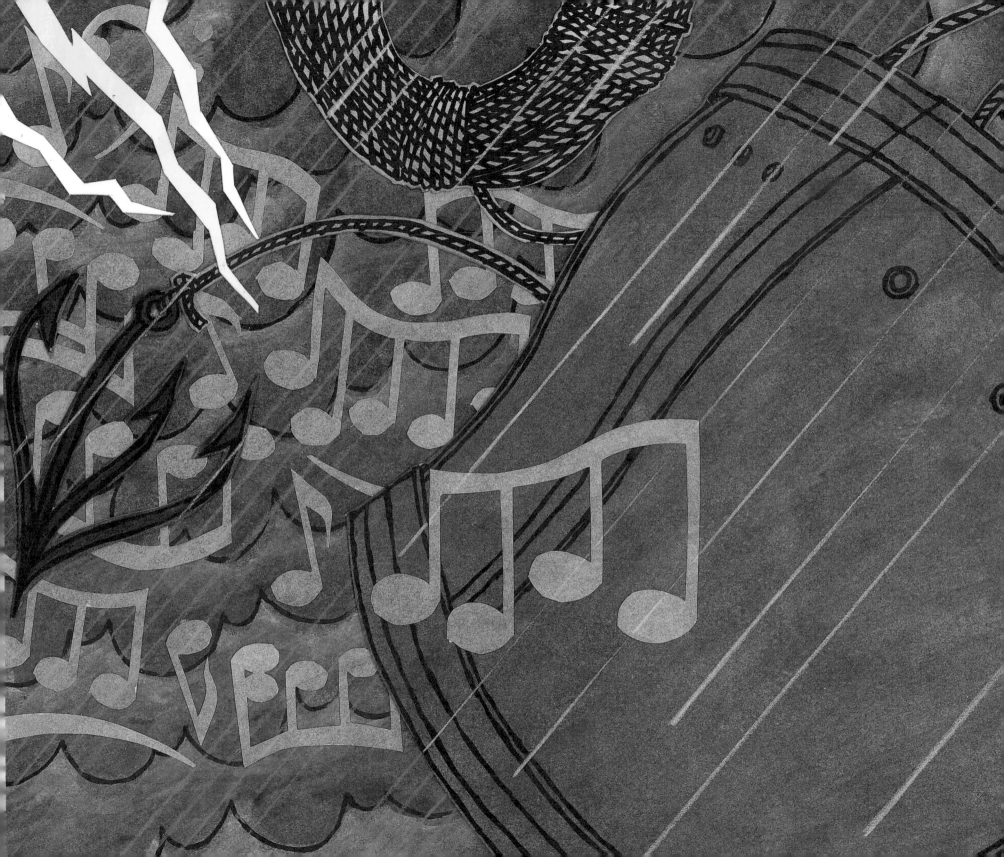

"Magic is fun!" said Freddie.

"And it tickles!" said Gingersnap.

They heard a song coming
from behind and sang along.

Suddenly, the storm stopped.

The rain vanished.

The winds blew away.

The clouds stood still.

Then something wonderful appeared . . .

. . . and the cloud hurried on its way.

As Freddie watched, something welled up inside,
and he started to sing.

"Well, look at that," Gingersnap exclaimed. . . .

"We found a cloud to keep, after all."

A CLOUD'S SONG

Words & Melody by Vincent X. Kirsch

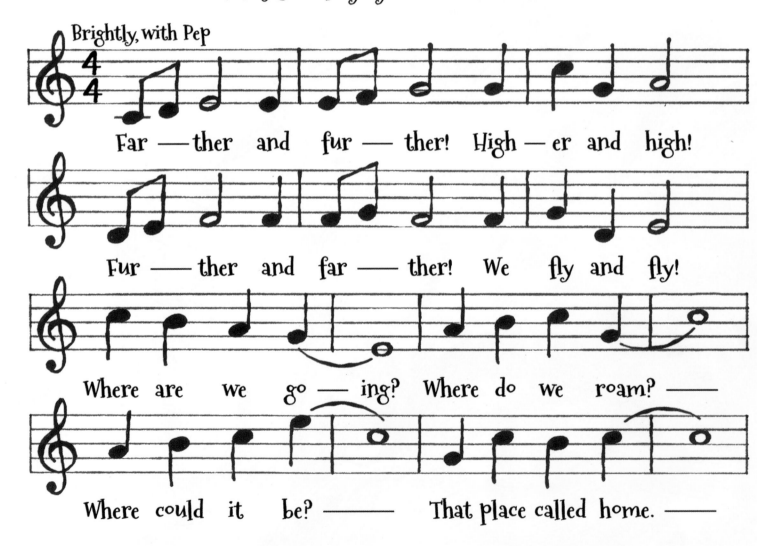